Samuel French Acting

Going To A Place Where You Already Are

by Bekah Brunstetter

SAMUELFRENCH.COM   SAMUELFRENCH.CO.UK

FOR PRODUCTION ENQUIRIES

UNITED STATES AND CANADA
Info@SamuelFrench.com
1-866-598-8449

UNITED KINGDOM AND EUROPE
Plays@SamuelFrench.co.uk
020-7255-4302

Each title is subject to availability from Samuel French, depending upon country of performance. Please be aware that *GOING TO A PLACE WHERE YOU ALREADY ARE* may not be licensed by Samuel French in your territory. Professional and amateur producers should contact the nearest Samuel French office or licensing partner to verify availability.

MUSIC USE NOTE

Licensees are solely responsible for obtaining formal written permission from copyright owners to use copyrighted music in the performance of this play and are strongly cautioned to do so. If no such permission is obtained by the licensee, then the licensee must use only original music that the licensee owns and controls. Licensees are solely responsible and liable for all music clearances and shall indemnify the copyright owners of the play(s) and their licensing agent, Samuel French, against any costs, expenses, losses and liabilities arising from the use of music by licensees. Please contact the appropriate music licensing authority in your territory for the rights to any incidental music.

IMPORTANT BILLING AND CREDIT REQUIREMENTS

If you have obtained performance rights to this title, please refer to your licensing agreement for important billing and credit requirements.

GOING TO A PLACE WHERE YOU ALREADY ARE premiered at South Coast Repertory Theatre in Costa Mesa, CA in March 2016. The performance was directed by Marc Masterson, with sets by Michael B. Raiford, costumes by Christina Wright, and lighting design by Tom Ontiveros. The Stage Manager was Jennifer Ellen Butler. The cast was as follows:

ROBERTA . . . . .Linda Gehringer

JOE . . . . .Hal Landon

ELLIE. . . . . .Rebecca Lynn Mozo

JONAS . . . . .Christopher Thorton

AN ANGEL. . . . . .Stephen Ellis

CHARACTERS

ROBERTA – sixty-six

JOE – seventy, her husband

ELLIE – thirties, Joe's granddaughter

JONAS – thirties, a stand-up in a wheelchair, and the irony is not lost on him

ANGEL/MAN/DOCTOR/CHECKOUT BOY – an ageless quality

SETTING

Heaven / Earth

TIME

Now

AUTHOR'S NOTES

Though one actor plays the **ANGEL**, the **MAN**, the **DOCTOR**, and the **CHECKOUT BOY**, they are meant to be played as fully formed, different characters. Treat it as a quadruple casting, with the similarity between the characters just being that the same human is inhabiting each of them.

Punctuation note: / indicates overlapping dialogue

For my Grandparents: living, dying, and already there:

Roberta Brunstetter
Richard Brunstetter
Jeannine Brunstetter
Beverly Bray
Joe Bray

A Funeral

*(**ROBERTA** and **JOE** sit in a pew in the back of a large church.)*

(They are tired, stiff, bored, but are feigning interest.)

(A nearly indecipherable voice speaks from the front: a voice of an old man through a microphone.)

VOICE OF PASTOR. "God be in my head and in my understanding; God be in my eyes, and in my looking; God be in my mouth and in my speaking; / God be in my heart, and in my thinking; God be at my end, and at my departing." Amen.

JOE. Really, "God be in my *mouth*"?

ROBERTA. I don't think he'd fit.

JOE. But he can fit anywhere, he's God.

ROBERTA. "God be in my sandwich."

JOE. "God: won't you please join me in my sock."

> *(**ROBERTA** laughs.)*

He has no mass, he has no *form*. He is an idea.

ROBERTA. *Shhhh.*

> *(A chorus of Amens. They mumble theirs, nearly apologetically, unaccustomed to saying it, as if called out.)*

JOE & ROBERTA. Amen.

> *(**ROBERTA** shifts in her seat, uncomfortably.)*
>
> *(Concerned.)* Your back bothering you?
>
> *(**ROBERTA** nods.)*

ROBERTA. Last time I bend down to pull up dandelions, I tell you *what.*

JOE. I bet you pinched / a nerve.

ROBERTA. I just tweaked it.

> *(But she shifts again.)*

JOE. Well then sit *still,* for Chrissakes.

ROBERTA. It's the pews. They make them so awful so you can't even fall asleep.

I remember slouching down in them. Drifting off till my mother pinched me awake.

> *(She remembers this, fully. It's a far-away feeling; happy, sad.)*

Church gives me feelings I can't stand.

Like I want to at the same time vomit and cry.

> *(Beat.)*

I want a cigarette.

JOE. You haven't had one in years.

ROBERTA. Church makes me want to smoke.

> *(**ROBERTA** shifts again in the pew, uncomfortable.)*

JOE. You shoulda brought the pillow.

ROBERTA. I don't need the pillow.

> *(Beat.)*

Whose funeral is this?

JOE. Hazel, from the office. Hazel.

> *(Beat.)*

ROBERTA. Didn't she already die?

JOE. To my knowledge, this is her first death.

VOICE OF PASTOR. And now a few words from Hazel's great-grandson, Jason.

> *(Sounds of **JASON** fumbling up toward the microphone, and fumbling with it just in general.)*

(He breathes through teen tears and the spit from his braces.)

VOICE OF JASON. Hi. Whoa. This is like crazy right now. My voice sounds so big.

JOE. Ahh, the eloquence of the youth.

VOICE OF JASON. Yeah, uh. Hazel was pretty cool. When I was little she was always touching my face and trying to hug me and give me bologna sandwiches. But then I like got old and started to see that she's pretty cool 'cause like, she's seen a lot of sh – stuff because to live to like ninety-three is like crazy like that's some cyborg shiz. But I'm glad I got to know her at all and stuff because you know like it's important to talk to your elders and get wisdom and learn from them and stuff and also now I get her accordion. And I bet she's up in heaven right now walking that weird little dog she had up and down Main Street, and he's just peeing everywhere and they're both like so happy.

JOE. So all dogs *do* go to heaven.

*(**ROBERTA** swats him, but also, she's laughing.)*

*(The **VOICE OF JASON** continues to drone on.)*

VOICE OF JASON. I'm gonna miss her a lot. And all the stuff she baked.

She made the best pound cake. Biscuits. Cobbler. Buttermilk cornbread. / Cheddar cornbread. Regular cornbread, apple pie, cherry apple pie – uh – yeah. That's all I can remember right now.

VOICE OF PASTOR. Thank you so much Jason. Thank you for those kind words.

ROBERTA. Well, now I want pie.

JOE. Mmmm, tell me about the pie.

ROBERTA. Warm peach, buttery crust, brown sugar, a la mode.

(They sit there, imagining this pie.)

JOE. We could stop at the diner on the way home.

ROBERTA. Well I can't actually *eat* that.

JOE. Says who?

ROBERTA. Says my girlish figure. Says my digestive system.

> (**JOE** *smiles, chuckles.*)
>
> (**ROBERTA** *fidgets again.*)
>
> (*The* **VOICE OF PASTOR** *drones.*)

She was still working? At ninety-*three*?

JOE. Part time. She used to answer the phones until her hearing went. Then she did the filing till her eyes started to go. She'd been working there for – seventy-three years?

ROBERTA. Well, Jesus, somebody should have just given her a retirement cake and sent her home.

> (*Beat.*)

Now I want cake –

JOE. We tried. She wouldn't listen.

ROBERTA. Or maybe she couldn't *hear*.

VOICE OF PASTOR. It's never easy, letting someone go. No matter how old. When we depart this earth, it is often sudden. Rarely do we get to say goodbye.

> (*Without looking at her,* **JOE** *takes* **ROBERTA**'s *hand.*)

ROBERTA. Was she a nice lady?

JOE. She was pleasant enough. She always took my pickles. Passing through the break room with my sandwich, she'd always take it. *I'll take that pickle off of you.* I really didn't know her all that well.

> (*Beat.*)

ROBERTA. Well wait a damn minute, what're we doing here if you didn't know her all that well?!

JOE. We are paying our respects.
The whole department is here. It's a required, ah. It's a social. You know. Expectation.

ROBERTA. "I didn't know you all that well, but you died, and so here I am."

>*(Beat.)*

I hate this.

JOE. Just try and sit still.

>*(Beat.)*

ROBERTA. *(Realizing.)* Oh God. We're old.

JOE. No we're not!

ROBERTA. We are! The old ones are dying so now *we* are the old ones.

JOE. We are medium-ish old, darling.

ROBERTA. Everyone is dying.

JOE. Well, yes, plants pass on, milk expires –

ROBERTA. I am not *milk*.

>*(Quieter.)*

I am not milk.

JOE. Okay, okay, you're not milk.

>*(Beat.)*

ROBERTA. This is what it is now, isn't it.
Funerals.
Remember when it was weddings? Birthday parties?
Swell reason to make friends.
I'll come to your funeral if you come to mine.

JOE. Well, if you go to someone's funeral they can't come to yours.

ROBERTA. I know. That's what we're going to do, now that we're old. We'll accumulate friends, so that when we look down at our bodies...

JOE. Look down from where?

ROBERTA. From wherever we are!

JOE. We're nowhere.

ROBERTA. I *know*, but if we *were* to be, just – let me finish, if we *were* to be somewhere –

JOE. Where?

ROBERTA. Somewhere –

JOE. We're here, and then we aren't, and that's that. Pulverem Pulvis.

> *(Beat.)*

ROBERTA. If you're so sure then what was the *Tibetan Book of the Dead* doing on your nightstand for months?

JOE. I must understand what I do not believe so that I can more thoroughly not believe it. And if I'm being honest, the book was dry, it was unfinishable.

> *(Beat. They listen.)*

I had a patient who swore he could become invisible / if he willed it so.

ROBERTA. You've told me this.

JOE. And I understood the emotion behind the impulse, yes, but of course it was not true.

It's a matter of physics. A human cannot lose their mass. / This is why we have *science*, so that people cannot go around saying they can make themselves transparent, just because the idea amuses them. I am not wrong.

ROBERTA. You've told me this!

You are wrong about / mustard, for one –

JOE. Roberta I do not like mustard, I will never like mustard.

ROBERTA. You're a goddamn idiot you are.

> *(Of church.)*

…Sorry.

JOE. Alright, where were we? When we look down at our bodies from God's massive lap, where we're perched, having assumed the body of a seven-year-old, ice cream in one hand, harp in the other, go on –

ROBERTA. We look down at our bodies.

And we see people crying –

Or moved to cry because all of the crying –

And you see all of the tears – and then it feels like it was worth it.

That it meant something.

JOE. What did?

ROBERTA. Being alive. For however many years. Doing what we did.

It was – worth it.

JOE. But what does it matter? Dust to dust. From flesh to food for the stars. And that is *that.*

> (**ROBERTA** *thinks. The thought troubles her.*)

ROBERTA. But –

JOE. But *what?*

> (*She wonders if that answer is enough for her.*)
>
> (*It's a large question that settles around her like dust.*)
>
> (*It's the sort of question that church brings.*)

VOICE OF PASTOR. …We take comfort in the knowledge that our lives here are temporary. On earth, we have fleeting moments of a surface sort of joy, then we are taken up to You, where we forever belong.

> (**ROBERTA** *starts to listen. To really listen.*)

ROBERTA. *Forever* forever?

JOE. So they say, kid.

ROBERTA. But what does that *mean?*

VOICE OF PASTOR. We take comfort in the knowledge that she was with us for a little while.

ROBERTA. Comfort…

VOICE OF PASTOR. But now she's with you. Forever.

JOE. And all of the unicorns.

And some sort of buffet.

With all of your favorites! Unlimited peel-and-eat shrimp.

ROBERTA. SHHHH!

VOICE OF PASTOR. "He will wipe away every tear from their eyes, and death shall be no more, neither shall there be mourning, nor crying, nor pain anymore, for the former things have passed away."

ROBERTA. *(Softly, to herself.)* ...No more...

VOICE OF PASTOR. Now if you would please join me in singing Hazel's favorite hymn.

> *(Everyone stands, so* **ROBERTA** *and* **JOE** *do too, in unison.)*
>
> *(Fumbling, they reach for hymnals underneath their seats.)*
>
> *(Fumble through the pages. Awkwardly, they sing.)*

SONG.
> COME, THOU FOUNT OF EVERY BLESSING,
> TUNE MY HEART TO SING THY GRACE,
> STREAMS OF MERCY, NEVER CEASING,
> CALL FOR SONGS OF LOUDEST PRAISE.

ROBERTA. I used to know this song – I used to sing this song –

> *(A* **MAN** *appears behind* **ROBERTA***. He is distant. Soft. But there. He watches her.)*

SONG.
> PRONE TO WANDER, LORD, I FEEL IT,
> PRONE TO LEAVE THE GOD I LOVE.
> HERE'S MY HEART, OH, TAKE AND SEAL IT,
> SEAL IT FOR THY COURTS ABOVE.

> *(Suddenly,* **ROBERTA** *starts to sob and sob, as if the sobs were ripped from her.)*
>
> *(***JOE** *has no idea what to do.)*
>
> *(His wife is not the kind to make a scene, or make a scene in public. He puts an arm around her.)*
>
> *(The* **MAN** *watches her with sympathy and understanding.)*

JOE. Hey, Bobs –

(**JOE** *tries to comfort her.*)

ROBERTA. Where is she going?

Where is she going to go?

(Suddenly, we see an **ANGEL***, glowing, watching, eyes focused on* **ROBERTA***.)*

(Longing to speak so he could give her an answer.)

JOE. The cemetery off Kirklees.

ROBERTA. But really.

Where are we going?

Where are we going to go?

A Connection

(**ELLIE** *is on her bed, lying on* **JONAS**.)

(*It's dusk.*)

(*They've been in bed for hours, kissing and exploring each other for the first time.*)

(*They both wear* **ELLIE**'s *comforter and not much else.*)

(*They're watching a video on* **JONAS**' *phone in which a famous comedian does stand-up about whether or not there is a God.*)

(**JONAS** *laughs.*)

(*He notices that* **ELLIE** *isn't.*)

JONAS. C'mon, you said you love Louie!

ELLIE. I do!

JONAS. Then what's wrong?

ELLIE. I just.

I don't like to laugh at God.

JONAS. Why not?

ELLIE. Because he can part oceans and bring down planes.

JONAS. Oh, I didn't realize that was him.

ELLIE. Yep. I'm pretty sure he actually feeds off of my fear and indecision, it makes him even more powerful.

JONAS. Oh, well that's a healthy presumption.

ELLIE. Thanks, I invented it myself.

(*Beat.*)

No but really. Don't you ever worry: what if He's real, and you don't believe in Him, and you're making jokes about Him, and one day He'll say *okay well fuck you, here, have all the cancer*?

JONAS. …Nope.

ELLIE. I just don't trust strangers. Including God.

JONAS. And yet, you have one in your bed right now.

ELLIE. You're not a stranger.

JONAS. Not anymore.

> *(Beat.)*

ELLIE. I just don't like to laugh at it. Him.

JONAS. No, you're right. It's not funny at all that there is a great man in the sky who thinks he's our dad and one day we get to go and live with our Cloud Dad.

ELLIE. I don't know if I believe in Cloud Dad. I haven't decided yet.

JONAS. You haven't *decided?*

ELLIE. Have you?

JONAS. Not definitively.

ELLIE. Well yes or no?

JONAS. I don't know. I don't know everything, I'm not God.

ELLIE. You're not?!

JONAS. Nope.

ELLIE. I like the way words leave your mouth.

> *(He kisses her, deep like they're both unlocking the safes around their secrets and thoughts. She pulls back. Lays her head on his chest.)*

JONAS. You are incredible.

> *(This freaks her out.)*

ELLIE. Sandwich!

JONAS. Hmm?

ELLIE. I want a sandwich.

JONAS. Tell me about the sandwich.

ELLIE. Rye bread, sharp cheddar cheese, fresh tomatoes, all shoved together and fried to death.

JONAS. Mmmmm.

ELLIE. Have we not eaten since last night?!

JONAS. We had that cereal?

> *(**ELLIE** nods, remembering.)*

I still can't believe you bought me dinner.

ELLIE. Uh, you forced me to. It was moral blackmail.

JONAS. I delicately suggested it and you were all, *ABSOLUTELY, here's a giant grassfed steak.*

ELLIE. I felt bad!

JONAS. Well, you should've! Hey do you steal people's social security checks, too?

ELLIE. No!

JONAS. Oh, so, parking in handicapped spots is your *main* form of asshole?

ELLIE. I told you! I didn't see the thing.

JONAS. The aggressively giant all-blue sign thing.

ELLIE. THREE MINUTES. I was in there for THREE MINUTES. Are we gonna keep doing this?

JONAS. Yep. Forever.

> (**JONAS** *smiles, wryly.*)

ELLIE. Okay, fine, if we're doing this, do you *always* lurk outside of grocery stores and wait for people to accidentally park in handicapped spots so you can yell at them?

JONAS. Nope. First time.

> (*Beat.*)

Meant to be.

> (*He smiles at her.*)

> (**ELLIE** *gets weirded out. Oh, hell no.*)

ELLIE. What time did we – when did we even get back here?

JONAS. Time is an illusion.

ELLIE. Okay that's – no. There is definitely such a thing as time.

I gotta get up.

I have work to do in the now part of time.

JONAS. No you don't.

ELLIE. Yes. I do.

> (*He pulls her back to bed.*)

(Kisses her, deep. She releases herself into it. But pulls back.)

This is. Um.

(Beat.)

I'm sorry if I'm. Being weird.

JONAS. I'm Jonas.

ELLIE. I remember your *name*.

(He pulls her toward him.)

(He burrows into her.)

(Her phones buzzes with a phone call.)

JONAS. You can get it.

ELLIE. No it's okay. It's my grandma. She can leave a message.

(She declines the call, starts to scroll through emails.)

(She reads, annoyed.)

JONAS. What tragedy beholds the world now?

ELLIE. My boss. I just got like ten emails from her.

Sorry – it's just –

(She reads the email, annoyed.)

I really have to –

Okay. The cuddle part is done. I really have work to do, you've gotta go.

JONAS. On a Saturday?

ELLIE. Yep, I've got to edit two articles and pretend I have five hundred words to say about "almond shaming."

JONAS. I could go get us some food while you work.

ELLIE. You really / don't have to –

JONAS. Stop talking. Start working. I'll get us dinner.

Could you grab me my chair?

(Beat.)

ELLIE. ...Sure.

(**ELLIE** *is suddenly deeply uncomfortable.*)

(*She's never "grabbed anyone's chair" before.*)

(*She reaches for clothes. Slips something on.*)

(*From the side of the bed wheels out* **JONAS**' *wheelchair.*)

Do I just bring it to you?

JONAS. If you could do a little dance with it first, that'd be awesome.

(*Then, off her look:*)

Bringing it to me would be great.

(*And she does.*)

Thanks.

(**JONAS** *gets dressed, moves himself into his chair with ease.*)

So what's almond shaming?

ELLIE. You don't wanna know and I don't wanna tell you.

JONAS. So you're a – what'd you say you are? An online society person?

ELLIE. Social media coordinator.

JONAS. It sounds like you just picked three words and put them together.

ELLIE. I do content, analysis, I generate and regurgitate layouts, posts –

JONAS. Ah. Cool.

(**ELLIE** *wants him gone. But he is still there, just smiling at her. Taking her in.*)

ELLIE. And you – transcribe –?

JONAS. Interviews, yep. Pays the bills.

I'm not proud.

Wait, yes I am.

ELLIE. ...It's cool, I shame almonds.

JONAS. And sometimes I do stand-up.

ELLIE. Comedy?

JONAS. Yep.

And no, the irony is not lost on me.

What're your feelings on Thai food?

ELLIE. You're so sweet, but.

I don't really wanna do the dinner and sleepover thing. If that's okay.

JONAS. I already slept over.

ELLIE. Well I don't want to do it again. This was a really nice, um. Series of moments but right now they have to end.

     (Beat.)

JONAS. That's cool. I get it.

What're you up to tomorrow night?

ELLIE. ...Working. It's going to be a busy week, um.

JONAS. Ah.

ELLIE. But thanks for – thanks.

JONAS. Hey: Thank *you.*

     (He heads for the door.)

ELLIE. It's not about the – it's not because –

JONAS. It never is.

     *(**ELLIE** reaches again for her phone to distract herself.)*

Good luck with your existential quandary.

ELLIE. Hmm?

     *(**JONAS** points up.)*

Oh. Yeah. Thanks.

JONAS. See you.

ELLIE. Do you need me to get the / door?

JONAS. Nope, I'm good.

ELLIE. Oh. Okay. Sorry.

Bye!

     (He goes.)

(JONAS *goes to the door. Opens it. Guides himself through. Then, he's gone.*)

(*The moment the door shuts,* ELLIE, *as if without oxygen, bursts across the room to her purse, violently rummages through it. Searching.*)

(*She finds a pack of cigarettes, pulls one out, puts it on the bed next to her, as she looks for a light. But she can't find her fucking lighter.*)

(*Rummages. Rummages.*)

(*Searches through pants pockets. Jacket pockets.*)

(*The* MAN *from the church appears. She doesn't seem to fully see or notice him.*)

(*He is more of a presence, that of mortality.*)

(*He goes to her. Takes the cigarette. Breaks it in half.*)

(*Puts it back where it was.*)

(ELLIE *finds her matches. Reaches for the cigarette.*)

(*Sees it's broken.*)

(*She reaches for another, lights it. Smokes.*)

(*Rushes to the window, shoves it open.*)

(*Lights the cigarette.*)

(*Breathes in deep.*)

(*Finally calms, as if just given a sedative, or air.*)

(*The* MAN *watches. Disapproving.*)

(ELLIE *leans against the window, smoking.*)

(*In… Out. In… Out.*)

(*Release.*)

A Routine Procedure

(**ROBERTA** *lays on a hospital bed, nervous, waiting.* **JOE** *sits in a chair nearby, also waiting.*)

JOE. Stop thinking about it.

ROBERTA. I'm not!

(*Beat.*)

JOE. STOP.

ROBERTA. Well what else is there to think about? They're gonna put me in a tube like a goddamn science experiment!

JOE. It's just an MRI, it's routine.

ROBERTA. I can't remember if I'm claustrophobic and I'm worried I'll find out when I'm in there.

JOE. You'll be *fine.* But don't fidget. You have to lie perfectly still.

ROBERTA. Well if you tell me not to fidget all I want to do is fidget.

What if I panic?

JOE. There's a panic button, should you panic.

ROBERTA. Am I going to?!

JOE. *No.*

ROBERTA. And you'll be here? The whole time?

JOE. I'll be right here.

(*Beat.*)

(*A* **NURSE** *enters, pops the wheels on her bed, starts to wheel her out.* **ROBERTA**'s *eyes grow wide with fear, but she tries to stay strong.*)

Be good, now.

ROBERTA. I will.

JOE. (*A joke.*) Don't die on me, now.

ROBERTA. Not yet.

JOE. (*An old routine.*) We're going to die simultaneously.

ROBERTA. They'll bury us in the same box.

(He waves goodbye.)

(He sits in a chair.)

(She is gone.)

(Time passes.)

(He falls asleep.)

(A heart rate monitor starts, beeping steadily.)

(And then, it flatlines.)

(Suddenly: the most glorious light you have ever seen. It overwhelms the space, blinding, pulsing, hugging, consuming. Then:)

Welcome

> *(Heaven.)*
>
> *(**ROBERTA** leaves her bed. She moves through time and space, through glory.)*
>
> *(Soft light. Every color ever.)*
>
> *(The **MAN**, who is now an **ANGEL**, greets her.)*
>
> *(He is overjoyed.)*

ANGEL. …Hi.

ROBERTA. Hi.

> *(**ROBERTA** looks at him.)*
>
> *(She can't place him. She can't remember what words are. What are words?)*
>
> *(She moves toward the **ANGEL**, searching for words, for recognition.)*

ANGEL. Wow. It's you. I, uh. OhmyGod. We say that here. Colloquially. It's totally fine. So.
Hi.

ROBERTA. I can't find my room. Or my house.
Or my. Anything.

ANGEL. This is in fact your room and house and also now your everything.

ROBERTA. …What?

ANGEL. I can't believe you're here.
We've been waiting a very long time for you.

ROBERTA. Where am I?

ANGEL. *(With wonder and authority.)* Heaven.

> *(With his announcement, clouds swell with beautiful music, then softly recede.)*

Pretty cool, right?

ROBERTA. I'm sorry, I think there's been some sort of mistake.

ANGEL. …Hmmm?

ROBERTA. My husband and I don't believe in heaven.

ANGEL. And yet, here you are! So WELCOME ROBERTA!

Sorry. That was too much.

I know it's a lot to process. Take your time, take it all in. I'm going to show you around, I'll be your guide until you get situated.

First and foremost, could you try and find words to describe how you feel, now that you're here? It's a survey thing we do. It's kind of my favorite thing, and I'm kind of in charge of it.

ROBERTA. I –?

ANGEL. Here's a few favorites.

"Being told you can smoke all the cigarettes you want and you'll never die."

"Like when you jump onto the Mario cloud but then you decide to live there."

Heh. Kids.

"That Camembert from Trader Joe's that's got a little bit of blue cheese inside of it."

"Salad of Color."

ROBERTA. *(Trying.)* …Frosting pillow fight.

ANGEL. There you go!

ROBERTA. Is there someone I could speak to – about –

ANGEL. You can speak to me.

ROBERTA. I don't understand why I'm here.

ANGEL. You will.

ROBERTA. What – what is that smell –

ANGEL. You know, little bit of this, little bit of that, fried chicken, waffles, childhood, just in general, lemon poppyseed muffins, your grandma's perfume, dryer sheets, homemade caramels –

ROBERTA. Is that – do I smell tater tots?

ANGEL. *(Proud.)* Yup! That was my suggestion. They've got parmesan cheese inside of them.

ROBERTA. It's beautiful –

ANGEL. Right? And you never get tired of smelling it, it's just like –

>   (*He sucks in air, hard.*)

And then it's like:

>   (*He exhales, deep.*)

But then again it's like:

>   (*He inhales, so deeply.*)

But then it's like –

ROBERTA. It's wonderful.

ANGEL. It is. Now, if you will just follow me –

ROBERTA. To where?

ANGEL. To begin.

ROBERTA. Begin what?

ANGEL. Forever.

>   (**ROBERTA** *looks around her.*)
>
>   (*The* **ANGEL** *just sort of – looks at her. In awe.*)
>
>   (*She breathes in.*)

ROBERTA. But –

Is Joe here, too?

ANGEL. No. He's not.

ROBERTA. Will he be here?

ANGEL. …I don't know.

>   (**ROBERTA** *feels a sudden pull to him, as his shape starts to form in her heart, pulling her back toward earth.*)

ROBERTA. Where is he?

>   (*Beat.*)

Where is he going to go?

>   (**ROBERTA** *looks back toward her Life.*)
>
>   (*She spots her hospital bed, empty,* **JOE** *waiting beside it.*)

(She moves back toward it.)
(For now.)

A Return

(Back in **ROBERTA***'s room. She is lying in her bed, unconscious.)*

*(***JOE*** waits by her side. He looks a wreck, like he's been crying.)*

(Finally, she wakes. He is overcome with joy and relief.)

JOE. Oh, thank God –

ROBERTA. What –

JOE. It's okay. It's all fine now.

(He kisses her forehead.)

ROBERTA. Where –

JOE. It all went fine. There were some – complications, but you're fine.

ROBERTA. Did I die?

JOE. No, sweetheart, you're right here.
You scared us for a minute, there. Welcome back.

ROBERTA. Welcome…

JOE. You want some water?

*(***ROBERTA*** looks around, confused.)*

ROBERTA. What –?

JOE. You got the MRI, but you had an allergic reaction to the dye, sweetheart, you went into shock – they gave you a sedative, you just took a nap.

ROBERTA. Where am I?

JOE. You're at the hospital.

*(***ROBERTA*** nods, processing.)*

ROBERTA. Am I here?

JOE. You're here.

(She looks at **JOE***. He chokes back a sob.* **ROBERTA** *sees this.)*

I'll get the – where is the doctor –

(He stands up to head out. **ROBERTA** *reaches for his arm, stopping him.)*

ROBERTA. I went to heaven.

(Beat.)

JOE. What?

ROBERTA. …Heaven.

(A moment as he processes.)

JOE. Okay –

ROBERTA. I was weightless, I was floating up, closer and closer to a light, a light that doesn't shine *on* but shines *through* –

JOE. Where is the nurse –
I – I don't – where is the button, where is the –

(Shouting, to hallway.)

NURSE!

ROBERTA. – up toward the bulb that was also the sun that was also a street light outside of a shopping mall? Up and up and up –

JOE. Okay, sweetheart –

(Pressing buttons, calling.)

Nurse!
Are you hungry? Do you want a yogurt?

ROBERTA. *(Declaring, a discovery.)* I want tater tots.
With parmesan cheese in the middle.

(The **ANGEL**, *who is now a* **DOCTOR**, *enters. He is cheerful, calm.)*

*(**ROBERTA** looks at him. He is vaguely familiar.)*

DOCTOR. I see we are awake.

ROBERTA. *(Searching.)* You –

JOE. She's awake, but she's tired, she's a bit confused. Is it alright to take her home to rest?

DOCTOR. Of course, of course. Nothing beats the glory of your own bed. But first:

(He stops. He clears this throat.)

I would like to first and foremost say that I am with you every step of the way. You are not alone.

JOE. What's this about?

DOCTOR. The results of Roberta's MRI.

*(The **DOCTOR** sits on a chair and slides himself closer to them.)*

*(He powers on a computer by the bed. Types on a small keyboard. Pulls up an image, which overwhelms the space. **ROBERTA**'s lungs. With a pen, he points to a large mass, the size of a baked potato.)*

JOE. …What's that?

DOCTOR. A tumor. Well, a series of tumors.

ROBERTA. It looks like a baked potato.

JOE. But – that's – she just had a pain in her back.

DOCTOR. Yes, well, that's where the tumors began, and then they seemed to have spread across multiple organs. Now of course I will need to do a biopsy, but based on their locations, I am fairly certain they are not benign.

JOE. *(Flummoxed.)* Well, we'd like to get a second opinion.

DOCTOR. Of course. But I will share with you: there are few things I am certain about, really truly certain. This is one of them.

*(**ROBERTA** keeps her eyes fixed on the fluorescent light above them, which seems to pulse. **JOE** reaches for her hand.)*

What we're looking at, here, are mediastinal tumors. They've formed in the cavity between your lungs. You see that this section here is pressing on the heart, and could eventually also cause pressure on the spine. Now I would like to go ahead and schedule a bronchoscopy, barium swallow and endoscopy to get a closer look, as well as a chest scan and additional MRIs.

(The **DOCTOR** *prattles on with medical terms.* **JOE** *tries to pay attention as* **ROBERTA** *just floats away.)*

The Arguments

(**ROBERTA**, *at home, on the couch. That evening.*)

(*She goes through a folder given to her by her doctor – pamphlets about chemo and alternative therapies.*)

(*She sets them down. She is still processing the news.*)

ROBERTA. I remember the first cigarette I smoked.

I was – thirteen?

(*Beat.*)

I was back behind the church with my older brother, Gregory, and a few of his friends, and they were talking, they were talking about something that I didn't understand and I felt a hole. I felt a hole in the moment. And I wanted to fill it and so I reached for one.

I'll take one a those.

Gregory lit it.

(*Beat.*)

There were other things I could've reached for.

(*Beat.*)

I did this to myself.

(*The thought kills her, nauseates her.*)

(**JOE** *enters from the kitchen, teapot in hand.*)

JOE. I've called into the office.

They've found me a replacement for tomorrow.

I've made some calls to some specialists, and Linda is also going to make some calls.

ROBERTA. Joe –

JOE. And I put a call into Dr. Dougherty. My colleague I was telling you about. He specializes in this sort of. He's just over in Fredrick. He's very busy, as the best are, but. I've left word for him, where's the mustard?

I can't find anything anywhere.

ROBERTA. Refrigerator door.

JOE. I already looked there.

ROBERTA. Well, that's the only place it is, it's mustard, where else would it be?

JOE. Well I don't know, I'm not usually in charge of the sandwiches!

ROBERTA. *(Standing.)* Well let me –

JOE. *(Firm.)* NO.

>   *(Beat.)*

No. I'll find it.

>   *(He starts to head back into the kitchen.)*

ROBERTA. Will you just sit here with me for a minute? You've been running around like a goddamn maniac.

JOE. I'm just trying to get your dinner.

ROBERTA. You won't even look at me.

JOE. *(Giving in, sitting with her.)* Fine.

See?

I'm sitting.

See? I'm looking at you.

>   *(He sits and looks at her. Tears start to come.)*

The water's boiling –

ROBERTA. No it's not.

>   *(She points to the kettle in his hand.)*

Do you not believe me? About heaven.

JOE. I don't not *believe* you, I just –

ROBERTA. Well then tell me what you think.

JOE. I don't want to get into this right now. You've had a long day.

ROBERTA. Come on. Give me your best shot. Therapy me.

>   *(Beat.)*

JOE. *(Gently.)* …There are studies.

I don't mean to belittle your, ah, but when the brain is deprived of oxygen, as yours was, ever so briefly – things shift.

ROBERTA. I wasn't high if that's what you're saying. "Oxygen."

JOE. Sweetheart. Listen to me. When there is trauma in the body, the mind sees what it wants. We are taken elsewhere. You remember when I had that young patient who was frightened of water? Nearly drowned, in Lake Michigan? He felt as if he'd been trapped under the boat for some five minutes. But when I asked his mother – not ten seconds he'd been under, she said, not ten. And what is the explanation?

ROBERTA. Don't talk to me like one of your students.

JOE. I am just trying to help you see.

The mind slows when it is processing trauma, creating an illusion of travel, of timelessness. You see? Time stretches out. Your heart stopped briefly, yes, but most likely your brain did not. And even if it did, just for a moment, the brain stem stays active. It's a primitive function, remnants of mammal behavior, of playing dead.

ROBERTA. I'm talking about a nice place where our souls go, is that so absurd?

JOE. It's a wonderful idea. But that's what it is. An *idea*.

(*Beat.*)

ROBERTA. But what if there's something up there?

JOE. Well of course there is. There is the *cosmos*, there is apparently *Pluto* –

ROBERTA. And maybe, also, there is a nice place that smells of waffle cones, where –

(**JOE** *doesn't know what to do. He laughs. This is absurd.*)

I don't think it's funny. I mean yes of course it is. But it's *not*.

JOE. ...I am just asking you to consider that perhaps, maybe, what you saw was a dream.

You went into shock, darling and you had a beautiful dream.

ROBERTA. ...You're probably right.

(*He kisses her forehead.*)

JOE. Now.

We're going to schedule your first appointment, get ahead of this. Now if you'll just tell me where your mustard is, I will see to your sandwich.

(*Beat.*)

ROBERTA. Look again. Where condiments live. Refrigerator door.

(JOE *heads back into the kitchen.*)

(ROBERTA *sits alone.*)

(*The phone rings.*)

Hello?

ELLIE. Roberta?

ROBERTA. Ellie! Ellie, I love you!

(ELLIE *exhales smoke.*)

ELLIE. (*Thrown.*) Oh – okay –

I was just gonna leave a message. I only have a minute. Lots of work.

Just calling you back.

Is now okay, or?

ROBERTA. Now is perfect. There is no better time than now.

ELLIE. Okay so. Now it is. Hi!

ROBERTA. Isn't it amazing, how there is right now, and there is then, and there is forever?

ELLIE. ...Yes?

(ELLIE *smokes.*)

ROBERTA. Are you smoking?

ELLIE. No.

> *(She starts to aimlessly pace.)*

So what's new? Why'd you call, or? I mean you can call whenever. But.

ROBERTA. I just wanted to say hi. See how you are.

ELLIE. Hi! I'm good.

> *(Beat.)*

ROBERTA. But well. Since then.

I went for an MRI.

> *(**ELLIE** smokes.)*

It was just for a pain in my back.

> *(**ROBERTA** finds her words.)*

And it turns out that I have a lot of tumors. All of the sudden.

Well they were probably growing for quite some time given their size but for me it's sudden because I didn't feel them growing at all.

> *(Beat.)*

ELLIE. Wait, so – *what?*

ROBERTA. They're in my lungs and a whole baked potato around my heart.

And well. It's not looking good.

> *(She takes a breath. Fights back tears.)*
>
> *(**ELLIE** smokes.)*
>
> *(Her heart leaps to her throat. She has no idea what to say.)*

ELLIE. Oh. Bummer.

> *(Beat.)*

I'm sorry. I have no idea why I just said "bummer," I never say that.

ROBERTA. No, you're right. It's a huge bummer.

Your granddad is calling specialists. Every doctor in a three hundred mile radius. I'm pretty sure he called a few veterinarians, too.

ELLIE. I'm so sorry – I don't know what to –

ROBERTA. Me neither.

ELLIE. Well are you going to – I mean –

ROBERTA. I don't know.

I've got to go now sweetie, there's another call coming in, bye bye.

ELLIE. Bye –

(*Quickly, she hangs up.*)

(**ROBERTA** *closes her eyes, trying to quiet the earthly noise, the worry.*)

(*She tries to go back. To summon every inch of what she remembers from being Up There.*)

(*The feel, the smell.*)

(*Softly the living room starts to pulse and glow.*)

(*Then:*)

(**ELLIE** *is smoking out the window, still processing the news.*)

(*A knock at her door.*)

(*She puts out the cigarette. Answers the door.*)

(**JONAS** *is there with a bag of food.*)

…What're you doing here?

JONAS. (*With a cinematic voice.*) "Rye bread. Sharp cheddar cheese. Fresh tomatoes. Shoved together and fried to death."

ELLIE. …What?

JONAS. "This summer – sandwiches will never be the same –"

ELLIE. ?

JONAS. I brought you a sandwich.

From this great spot right across the street from my place. It's called Sandwich.

Technically I brought one for both of us. Remember the –?

(Beat.)

ELLIE. I'm working right now, so –

JONAS. I know, but I'm a terrible listener and also incredibly persistent, so you're shit outta luck.

(He smells the air.)

Do you smoke?

ELLIE. *(An old excuse.)* Nope! It's from the apartment upstairs.

JONAS. Ah.

I just thought maybe you might want a break. From the work.

ELLIE. I can't take a break.

JONAS. From shaming almonds? Yeah you can.

ELLIE. I am never not doing anything. I don't ever not have plans. I do not have the luxury of free time. I work from home, so I am always working. If I am not doing something it's because I am not doing anything on *purpose*. And if I don't have plans to go anywhere or do anything, it's probably because I planned to not do anything and to stay in and work, which means I do have plans, which is to *work*.

JONAS. *(Amused.)* Got it.

ELLIE. I know I sound insane but I juggle a lot and it's the only way I can get it all done.

JONAS. I'll get *you* all done.

ELLIE. *(A small eruption.)* What is wrong with you?! Why do you like me, I am being so mean to you!

JONAS. …I just / do.

ELLIE. I'm not gonna date you, I am not your girlfriend, I am not gonna be your wife!

JONAS. Okay, Jesus!

> *(Beat.)*

ELLIE. I just don't know how – this – could ever. Um.

JONAS. You had a lot of sex with me for a person that you do not "know how this could ever, um."

ELLIE. That doesn't mean –

> *(Beat.)*

You don't want me. I promise you.

I have no moral code.

I barely like dogs.

My grandma just told me she's dying and I felt nothing.

Except the feeling of not feeling what I was supposed to feel.

JONAS. The one who called the other night?

ELLIE. Yeah.

JONAS. Oh man. I'm so sorry.

ELLIE. See? That was great, how'd you do that?

JONAS. Do what?

ELLIE. Say that with such sincerity.

I can't even do that.

See? I' m telling you. Shitty person.

JONAS. No. You're not.

You have this like kindness that's –

ELLIE. What is this "kindness"? That I've never lit anyone's house on fire, is that what is now called "kindness," what're you *talking* about?

JONAS. You went out in the rain and got us Cinnamon Toast Crunch because I said my mom used to give it to me when I was sick.

ELLIE. *(Erupting.)* Because I needed a cigarette!!

JONAS. I thought you said you didn't smoke.

ELLIE. I LIED. I am a liar and I am violently addicted to nicotine!

JONAS. You think that makes you a shitty person?

ELLIE. Okay, I felt weird with you in public. How about that?

    (There it is.)

JONAS. Oh. Well, you'll get over that. Trust me.

ELLIE. I don't know if I can.

    (Beat.)

I don't deserve you. You're a really good person, and –

JONAS. Oh, really?

ELLIE. And I'm just. I'm not a good enough person to be with you. With all the…

JONAS. Just stop.

You think you're a bad person because you just admitted that having dinner with me made you feel uncomfortable? Because if so, guess who else is a piece of shit? Every single other person. But you know what is *actually* shitty? Assuming that just because I'm in this chair I am a goddamn saint. Because I'm not. I am an asshole. Sometimes I ghost on women just to show them that I can. I use my chair to get free stuff. In high school I used to shoplift from Goodwill. People are not wholly good or wholly bad. I am not a "really good person" any more than anyone else is. And it is shitty and simplistic to not allow me to be any other way.

ELLIE. I'm sorry – I wasn't trying to –

    (Beat.)

JONAS. Maybe you're right. Maybe you are a shitty person.

ELLIE. But I'm trying not to be.

JONAS. Yeah, keep on telling yourself that. Maybe one day it'll be true.

    (He goes. Shuts the door behind him, hard.)

    *(**ELLIE** is left alone with the truth.)*

    (She reaches for a cigarette.)

Wisdom

(The next afternoon.)

*(***ROBERTA*** *is going through boxes of old papers and books that the ***ANGEL*** has laid out for her, unbeknownst to her.)*

(The air is thick with ink and dust.)

*(***JOE*** *enters from outside, where he's been working in the yard.)*

*(He is surprised to find ***ROBERTA*** awake.)*

JOE. I thought you were going to take a nap?

ROBERTA. I couldn't sleep.

JOE. Did anyone call?

ROBERTA. No.

JOE. I got the rest of the dandelions! In a few weeks we can plant some freesia. Then come summertime, full bloom!

      *(***ROBERTA*** *just nods.)*

What's all this?

ROBERTA. I'm going through the boxes from the garage. Look at this.

      (She hands him a matchbook.)

      (He inspects it.)

JOE. *(Smiling.)* Murphy's? What a shithole.

ROBERTA. It was *our* shithole.

Remember me then? After Charlie?

JOE. Of course.

ROBERTA. I felt defective. Like you found me in a bin at a discount store.

JOE. 1985.

ROBERTA. Eighty-*six*.

You picked me up.

JOE. We picked each other up.

ROBERTA. We were the oldest people there. We had to.

JOE. Couple a grown ups.

ROBERTA. You were so embarrassed that you were forty and just in school.

JOE. You kept apologizing that you were "just a dental secretary."

ROBERTA. You kept telling me that was nothing to be ashamed of, that a good secretary was hard to come by.

JOE. And you kept insisting that you were *not* a good secretary.

ROBERTA. You kept insisting your wife didn't leave you, you left *her.*

JOE. We left each other.

ROBERTA. I still smoked then.

JOE. I pretended like I didn't mind.

> *(She reaches for his hand. Kisses it.)*
>
> *(Beat.)*
>
> *(And she puts the matchbook into the trash.)*

JOE. Is that the trash?

> *(He starts to dig the matchbook back out.)*

ROBERTA. I'm cleaning up. I have too much stuff, we don't need all this stuff.

JOE. Sit down. You're supposed to be resting.

ROBERTA. No, this needs to be done.

JOE. Why?

ROBERTA. A realtor is coming tomorrow.

JOE. Why?

> *(She takes a breath. She knows this will be hard to say, even harder to hear.)*

ROBERTA. I thought it'd be a good idea to have a realtor / come and look at the house. Just in case we need to – she's a friend of Jill's –

JOE. You called a realtor?!

ROBERTA. I called Jill to tell her. And she did the same when her father –
This house is too big for just you. And I don't want to think about you here all alone.

JOE. Roberta, that's – we're not even *there*.

ROBERTA. I looked up some places. There's one with a lake. You could feed the ducks.

JOE. I don't want to feed the ducks!
I – I don't agree with this.

> *(He starts to pull things back out of the trash bag, each book and letter, with great care.)*

ROBERTA. *(Tired.)* Joe – I'm just trying to make things easier for you.

JOE. Is this because of your dream?

> *(**ROBERTA** is silent.)*

That's all it was, it was a *dream.*

> *(Beat.)*

ROBERTA. *(An admission.)* I still pray, sometimes.

JOE. What? When?

ROBERTA. Every now and then.

JOE. Well. I've never seen you do it.

ROBERTA. Well, you're not in my head.

JOE. Well, thank God.

ROBERTA. I would pray / when you flew for work.

JOE. Prayer is just wishful thought.

ROBERTA. *Dear God. Please keep Joe in the air and then put him safe back on the ground again.*

JOE. Did he ever answer?

ROBERTA. Well, are you dead?

JOE. Not that I know of.

ROBERTA. Well, there you go. And we have prayer to thank.

JOE. No, we have aerodynamics, we have aerodynamics to thank.

ROBERTA. See, this is why I kept it to myself.

JOE. Call Jill. Have her cancel the – the house is not for sale.

>   *(Beat.)*

ROBERTA. Maybe that's why I went. Because I pray.

JOE. Sweetheart, you didn't go anywhere.

ROBERTA. How do you know?

JOE. So, what? You subscribe to the ways of the Bible, now?

ROBERTA. I – I don't know –

JOE. You believe that we should own slaves. Eat our children.

ROBERTA. I'm not talking about that, I'm talking about a nice place / where –

JOE. You don't get to pick and choose.

ROBERTA. You can't even – just for me – consider that / maybe

JOE. No, I cannot. You are smarter than this.

ROBERTA. It's got nothing to do with my *intelligence.*
I know I haven't read as many books as you but maybe I have a thing that is called "emotional intelligence" and maybe I can perceive what is true.

JOE. This is ridiculous.

ROBERTA. You're the smartest person I ever met. That's the truth. But you can't have the simplest conversation about something meaningful with someone you love.

>   *(Angrily, she puts something else in the trash.)*
>
>   *(He pulls it back out.)*
>
>   *(He starts to pull everything out of the trash bag. It becomes desperate.)*

(Melting.) Joe.

Joe, I know you can hear me.

>   *(Beat.)*

Joe, your hearing aid's off.

JOE. *(Giving in to an old joke.)* I don't wear a hearing aid.

ROBERTA. *(Firm.)* I am just making plans. Please let me make some sort of plan.

JOE. We *have* a plan. Dr. Dougherty owes me a call back, Martin said he checked in with him, and that he's going to *call.*

ROBERTA. But if I go –

JOE. YOU WON'T.

ELLIE. Roberta?

> *(The voice feels far.)*
>
> **(ROBERTA** *turns and looks at* **ELLIE,** *standing in the doorway. She holds a horrendous bouquet of flowers.)*

ROBERTA. Ellie?

ELLIE. Hi –

ROBERTA. Ellie!!

> **(ROBERTA** *goes to* **ELLIE,** *wrapping her arms around her.* **ELLIE** *is a bit uncomfortable in* **ROBERTA***'s arms.)*

ELLIE. These are for you. They're from the airport.

ROBERTA. They're beautiful.

> *(**ELLIE** spots **JOE.**)*

ELLIE. Hi, Grandpa.

JOE. Hello, Ellie.

> *(She gives him a tentative, obligatory hug. They are not close, or comfortable around each other.)*

ELLIE. How are you?

JOE. Fine, fine, the grass is growing back in the front yard, I'm fine, the azaleas are blooming.
Your hair is long.

> *(They have no idea how to relate with each other, yet they are bursting with love for each other that they cannot express.)*

ELLIE. It is!

ROBERTA. Look at you, you're beautiful – You're here –

ELLIE. I'm here. Surprise! I can't stay long, but...

JOE. *(Attempting.)* ...Philly must still be cold this time of year!

ROBERTA. She's in Chicago, now.

JOE. Right, right, of course. Colder!

ELLIE. Yup, very cold!

ROBERTA. I wish you'd called, there's barely any food in the house.

ELLIE. Oh, it's okay –

> *(Beat. They all just kind of stand there, unaccustomed to being in a room alone together. It maybe happens once a year and there's usually a Christmas tree to stare at and talk about.)*

JOE. I'll go get some food.

ROBERTA. Joe, don't run off, say hello to your granddaughter!

JOE. *(To* **ELLIE.***)* Hello.

> *(He reaches for his coat, and goes.* **ROBERTA** *and* **ELLIE,** *alone.)*

> *(***ELLIE** *reaches into her bag, looks for an outlet.)*

ELLIE. I just need to charge my phone.

ROBERTA. Behind the lamp.

> *(***ELLIE** *plugs in her phone.)*

It's silly when you step back and – above. There are so many different types of lamps but they all make the same light. They're all just one thing.

ELLIE. ...Right!

> *(***ELLIE** *stands near her phone like it's her baby on life support.)*

I didn't bring my computer or anything, I really wanted to shut down, not think about work, and just be here, so.

But I need to have my phone. So.

ROBERTA. ...You never call me Grandma. I'm married to your grandfather.

ELLIE. Grandma Bonnie was weird about me calling you Grandma.

ROBERTA. Well, she's dead now.

> *(Beat.)*

God rest her soul.

May her soul rest. In the –

ELLIE. Yeah.

ROBERTA. And so I'm your grandma.

ELLIE. Okay. Sorry, yeah.

> *(Beat.)*

I'm glad you're, ah. I'm glad you still have some time. With us.

ROBERTA. Me too. Your granddad isn't taking it very well.

ELLIE. Yeah, I bet. Not.

> *(Beat.)*

Sorry. I don't know what you're supposed to say. When this stuff, ah. Transpires.

ROBERTA. Yep. Me neither.

> *(Beat.)*

ELLIE. ...How're you feeling?

ROBERTA. Little tired. But other than that, alive.

ELLIE. Oh.

Weird.

Cool.

Yay.

> *(Beat.)*

"I wish I had the right words for you. Just know I care."

> *(**ROBERTA** smiles at her. Nearly laughs.)*

ROBERTA. What the hell was that?

ELLIE. On the plane I looked up what to say and what not to say. In these situations. There were a lot of different – That was the one I remembered and so I said it.

ROBERTA. What're you not supposed to say?

ELLIE. "You're going to a better place," "Be strong…"

ROBERTA. Why wouldn't you tell someone that they're going to a better place?

ELLIE. I don't know, because maybe it's not true?

(*Beat.*)

ROBERTA. How's your mom and dad?

ELLIE. Uh, fine. Still married. Still breathing air.
They want to come, but –

ROBERTA. I'm not their mother.

(*Beat.*)

ELLIE. I made that pineapple upside-down cake that you gave me the recipe for!

ROBERTA. You did? How'd it turn out?

ELLIE. Great. I felt like a real-live girl.

ROBERTA. That's really all it takes to be a woman in this world today. Just bake the occasional cake, succumb to that expectation. But other than that just do what you want and say whatever it is that you want. Or at least that's how I decided to live.

ELLIE. I like that.

ROBERTA. (*Realizing.*) I have another recipe you have to try.

(*She searches for her glasses, finds them, then starts to search through magazines.*)

It's a vegetable lasagna, but you use zucchinis instead of the noodles, it's better for you. You have to try it, it is to DIE for –

ELLIE. HA!

(*Then.*)

Sorry.

ROBERTA. Ha. We're funny.

It's somewhere – it's somewhere –

(She looks and looks. Loses herself a bit.)

Too many magazines!

I can't find the…

ELLIE. It's okay. Maybe it's online.

ROBERTA. But I have the clipping, it's somewhere.

It's somewhere. There are too many things.

*(**ROBERTA** just – sits, surrounded by magazines. For the tiniest of moments, she is a baby again, confused by the mess she's just made.)*

And it all just goes away.

*(**ELLIE** isn't sure what to do. Looks in the box.)*

(Finds a picture.)

ELLIE. Is that you and Grandpa?

ROBERTA. It is.

*(**ELLIE** looks through them, mesmerized.)*

Would you like to – have some of them?

ELLIE. Uh – sure. I mean yes! Yes. I love old things.

ROBERTA. Hey!

ELLIE. Not that you're –

I mean things that are old.

ROBERTA. I do, too.

I'll pick some good ones out for you.

*(**ELLIE** spots a framed picture on an end table.)*

(She picks it up.)

ELLIE. Where'd you get this?

ROBERTA. Oh! It's from when you finished that marathon!

ELLIE. It was just a half marathon.

ROBERTA. But still. It's impressive.

ELLIE. Aw. Thanks.

ROBERTA. The longest I ever ran was a mile. And I stopped in the middle of it to smoke. Ha!

ELLIE. Did my mom send it to you?

ROBERTA. I think I printed it offline.

> *(This stabs at* **ELLIE***'s heart. She puts the picture back down.)*

Are you still running?

ELLIE. No.

> *(Beat.)*

I gave up.

ROBERTA. Hard on the knees.

ELLIE. Yep.

ROBERTA. So are you seeing anyone?

ELLIE. Not really. No one. I'm a shitty person, so, hard to find a, match.

ROBERTA. No you're not.

You came to see your grandma, didn't you?

> *(***ELLIE*** fights back tears that surprise her.)*
>
> *(She thinks of* **JONAS***.)*
>
> *(She tries to push this out. But she can't.)*
>
> *(She dissolves into tears.)*

ELLIE. I'm sorry, I'm sorry –

ROBERTA. Sweetie?

ELLIE. You're dying and I'm crying in your house –

ROBERTA. Oh honey. Please don't cry over a boy, or lack thereof. They are not worth it. The only things worth crying over are flat tires and tax returns. And the occasional Baptist hymn.

ELLIE. That's not why I'm – well it is, but – It's not *just.*

ROBERTA. Whatever it is, it's alright –

> (**ROBERTA** *pulls her into her arms, comforts her.*
> **ROBERTA** *herself feels needed. Which in itself is*
> *comforting.*)

ELLIE. I feel like I'm not doing life right. I'm wasting it.

ROBERTA. There's no such thing.

> (*She comforts her.*)

But I felt the same when I was your age.

ELLIE. You did?

ROBERTA. Absolutely.

ELLIE. Does it go away?

ROBERTA. No. Not really. I think it's just part of being alive.

> (**ELLIE** *nods.*)
>
> (*Dries her tears.*)
>
> (*Goes to a box of old things.*)
>
> (*Starts to dig through.*)
>
> (*Finds another picture. Loves it instantly.*)

ELLIE. Oh my God. Is this you?

ROBERTA. Yes it is! Got that coat with my first real paycheck. Called it my "grown-up coat."

ELLIE. Please tell me you still have it.

ROBERTA. I do somewhere. If I can find it, it's yours.

ELLIE. Oh – you don't have to –

ROBERTA. It's yours.

> (*Beat.* **ELLIE** *smiles.*)

ELLIE. Okay.

> (*She digs again through the box. Finds a small,*
> *clear envelope with a tiny bracelet inside.*)

…What's this?

> (**ROBERTA**'s *face softens. Sinks into memory. She*
> *holds her hand out.* **ELLIE** *gives it to her.*)
>
> (*After a few moments:*)

ROBERTA. …It was Charlie's.

ELLIE. Who's Charlie?

ROBERTA. My son.

ELLIE. I didn't know you had a son.

ROBERTA. I don't. I do. I did. He passed away, when he was very young.

> *(Beat.)*

I smoked all through my pregnancy.

I've never said that out loud before.

ELLIE. Was he your and – Grandpa's?

ROBERTA. No.

I met your grandfather after, it. I was very damaged, it was very sexy.

I didn't have a relationship. With the father.

But.

Being a woman of a certain age, I… I decided to keep him. And I carried him, and then I had him, and he was – broken. He was barely a person but a full person to me, with a name and a nature. I lived with him for three months in a tiny room with things beeping and numbers going. And then he died.

> *(**ELLIE** takes her hand.)*

And I carried that guilt around. Like a big wet dress I was forced to wear. My whole life.

Your grandpa made me feel it less, but. I always had it.

But there – it was gone.

> *(Beat.)*

ELLIE. Where?

> *(**ROBERTA** looks at **ELLIE**.)*
>
> *(Decides to tell her.)*

ROBERTA. …Heaven.

I went to heaven.

ELLIE. When?

ROBERTA. When I was in the machine. At some point in there or after.

(*Beat.*)

ELLIE. I thought you and Grandpa were atheists.

ROBERTA. We were. He is. I'm not – I was. Which worked just fine for me, for some time.

(*Beat.*)

I didn't used to be. When I was young, I believed. In.

(*Beat.*)

It was probably a dream.

Or hallucination.

Your granddad printed off some articles. To help me understand what may have happened.

There are explanations.

When the eye is deprived of blood.

When endorphins are released.

When something called the temporo something junction is stimulated.

The brain becomes a cinema.

(*Beat.*)

Best movie I ever saw.

(**ROBERTA** *hears the music.*)

(*It sucks her back. Vivid, real.*)

ELLIE. What was it like?

(**ROBERTA** *settles in to tell.*)

(*She closes her eyes, taking herself back there, straining to remember, letting the feeling of being there overwhelm her.*)

ROBERTA. …My limbs were like marshmallows.

The big kind you bring for camping? Yes, that kind.

There were – gates. Far away but I could see them. I felt like if I took one step forward I would be through them. And there was someone assigned to me.

He seemed like he'd been next to me my whole life.

And there was a smell all around like deep fried vanilla.

(She seems to get transported back there as she remembers.)

And I felt so light because – my regrets had been lifted. The weight of everything I hadn't done right. It pulls us *down*. It's not gravity, it's regret. And I could feel it all *gone*. And so I went up and up –

(Beat.)

All my life I've ached with a question.

Being there felt like the answer.

(Beat.)

Do you think it was real? That it could have been?

ELLIE. I don't know.

Maybe.

ROBERTA. Maybe? You think?

ELLIE. Maybe.

(She brings a hand to the couch.)

(It feels foreign, strange, cold.)

ELLIE. I'm going to make you some tea, okay?

ROBERTA. Hmm?

ELLIE. Tea.

*(**ROBERTA** nods.)*

*(**ELLIE** goes into the kitchen.)*

*(**ROBERTA** sits, alone.)*

*(The **ANGEL** appears.)*

*(**ROBERTA** fixates on him.)*

ANGEL. You left so soon. I didn't get to give you your welcome gift! It's protocol. Here.

(He hands her a perfect ice cream cone.)

ROBERTA. Is this real?

ANGEL. Try it.

(She takes a lick.)

(Holy shit.)

ROBERTA. What flavor is this?

ANGEL. It's got bits of the birthday cake your grandma used to make you. It's whipped with clouds and a couple of lazy afternoons.

(She takes another.)

(Dear God.)

(She closes her eyes with worship.)

(She savors, she enjoys.)

You love ice cream.

ROBERTA. I do. I spend so much energy pretending like I don't but I do.

It's the only thing that I love purely. And Joe. Most of the time.

ANGEL. You would wake up, 4 a.m.

Stomach rumbling.

You were hungry but not for meat.

For sugar and milk.

You'd get those big tubs from the grocery store.

Neapolitan.

You'd take the scooper across all three parts into a coffee mug.

*(**ROBERTA** is stunned.)*

ROBERTA. …Charlie?

ANGEL. That's me!

ROBERTA. CHARLIE?!

ANGEL. Hi Mom.

*(The **ANGEL** nods.)*

(**ROBERTA**'s *face moves from shock to joy. She smiles. Joy for the first time. Joy like Nutella, like new pillows, like fresh, warm bread.*)

ROBERTA. My boy –

You're all grown up!

ANGEL. I wanted to talk to you. So many times.

ROBERTA. Me too – I talked to you, so many nights –

ANGEL. Sometimes I turned on that lamp.

ROBERTA. That was you?!

(*The* **ANGEL** *nods.*)

(*Hand to her heart, her gut.*) You never left. I kept you right here.

ANGEL. I know.

ROBERTA. Tell me everything about you. I want to know everything.

…What's your favorite color?

No, what's your favorite food?

No – are you happy?

ANGEL. Uh, yellow, ice cream *duh*, and BIG TIME.

ROBERTA. Me too, me too!

Do you have friends, do you play an instrument, have you ever been in love?

ANGEL. Yes, harp, yes I have.

ROBERTA. What's she like? The girl?

ANGEL. …He.

ROBERTA. Oh!

ANGEL. Yep.

ROBERTA. So you're –

ANGEL. A gay angel. A gayngel if you will.

ROBERTA. I will.

ANGEL. I like to make up words and try and get them going on earth but it like never works.

ROBERTA. I wouldn't have minded. That you –

ANGEL. I know.

>> *(Beat.)*
>>
>> *(Of her ice cream cone.)*

May I?

ROBERTA. Sure.

>> *(She hands him her cone.)*
>>
>> *(He takes a giant, happy lick.)*

It wasn't a dream, was it?

ANGEL. Sometimes the truth doesn't jive with physics and then it's like *(Mimes brain exploding.)* but personally that's exactly where I like to be. I have a curious nature.

ROBERTA. So do I.

>> *(Beat.)*

…No one believes me. That I went.

ANGEL. …They never do.

ELLIE. *(Offstage.)* Hey, where's your honey?

>> *(**ROBERTA** turns to look toward the kitchen.)*
>>
>> *(When she turns back – the **ANGEL** is gone.)*

Grandma?

>> *(**ROBERTA** keeps her eyes fixed on the space the **ANGEL** once held.)*
>>
>> *(Suddenly, a peace washes over her.)*
>>
>> *(She is joyful, dazed.)*

A Gesture

(**ELLIE** *is hiding outside of her grandparents' house, smoking furtively.*)

(*She makes a call.*)

(**JONAS**, *somewhere else. He looks at his phone, surprised to see her calling with her voice, and surprised to see her calling, at all.*)

JONAS. *(Answering.)* Hi.

(*Beat.*)

ELLIE. Hi.

Thanks for answering.

JONAS. ...Sure.

(*Beat.*)

ELLIE. So what's up, asshole?

JONAS. Hmm?

ELLIE. You're an asshole, remember? You asshole.

(*Beat.*)

Remember you said –

JONAS. Yep, I remember.

(*Beat.*)

ELLIE. How're you?

JONAS. Freezing my ass off, my heat's broken.

ELLIE. You wanna go crash at mine?

JONAS. You're not there?

ELLIE. I'm at my grandparents' house.

JONAS. How's she doing?

(**ELLIE** *tears up at the thought of what she's about to say.*)

ELLIE. Well she's dying. Full of cancer. All up in her, so. These are not technical terms.

JONAS. I'm sorry –

ELLIE. It's okay, it's fine, she's had a good life and everything, I don't know why I'm crying.

(Beat. They breathe.)

JONAS. So…

ELLIE. I don't wanna be a bad person.

JONAS. I think the fact that you don't wanna be means that you're *not*.

(Beat.)

ELLIE. How do you do that?

I can't even speak in full sentences, and you're just – so –

JONAS. Constantly saying the exact thing that you need to hear by means of intuition?

ELLIE. Yeah.

JONAS. It's called intuition.

ELLIE. My grandma says she saw heaven?

JONAS. Like –?

ELLIE. Yeah.

(Beat.)

JONAS. That's awesome. Maybe she did.

ELLIE. So wait, you think it's there?

JONAS. Why would I *not* want to regain control of my limbs and then also live forever?

ELLIE. But then, so is there also a hell?

JONAS. Yep. It's just a place where they make you stand in really long lines and listen to lots of Creed. Or it's possible we all just turn into sand.

ELLIE. Maybe.

I don't *not* believe her. But. That feels like a cop out. You know? Don't I need to decide?

JONAS. There's the operative word. "Decide."

ELLIE. …Yeah.

JONAS. "A human being is a deciding being."

ELLIE. Who said that?

JONAS. Me. Just now.

> *(Beat.)*

And also Viktor Frankl.

ELLIE. Ah.

I can't tell if she's just being crazy, but I don't want her to think I think she's crazy, because she's going to die soon, and these are fragile moments, and –

Ha, This is, ah, and this is turning into a way more emotional, ah, than I meant it.

I should go.

JONAS. You don't have to.

ELLIE. Okay.

> **(JONAS** *is quiet. Grins into the phone.)*
>
> *(He knows he's nearly won.)*

…What?

JONAS. You're thinking about me so hard right now.

> **(ELLIE** *can't help it. She smiles again.)*

ELLIE. Cause I'm on the phone with you!

JONAS. You wanna have all of my little paraplegic babies.

ELLIE. No I *don't!*

> *(She does.)*

JONAS. …When're you back?

ELLIE. Tomorrow.

> *(Beat.)*

So I'll see you tomorrow?

JONAS. Actually, I don't have the luxury of free time –

ELLIE. *(Come the fuck on.)* Really?

JONAS. *(Smiling.)* See you tomorrow.

ELLIE. Yeah.

G'night.

JONAS. G'night.

(But neither hangs up.)

ELLIE. You're still there.

JONAS. So're you.

ELLIE. So're you.

(They smile into their phones, breathing into each other.)

(A few moments of rest.)

ELLIE & JONAS. G'night.

(They hang up. Both floating with feeling.)

*(**ELLIE** goes inside.)*

A Shift

(Morning.)

(JOE is setting out breakfast – a plate of bacon, a plate of eggs. ELLIE enters, ready to go, toothbrush in hand.)

JOE. Morning!

ELLIE. Hi!

JOE. I've got breakfast, here, ah – bacon – this is the good kind, it's turkey bacon, but I crisp it. At least I think it's the turkey bacon. Do you like bacon?

ELLIE. Yeah! I'm usually vegan, but this is fine.

(She grabs a few pieces. Eats as she zips her toiletries into her bag.)

JOE. Have you seen a pair of glasses? I can't find my glasses –

ELLIE. I haven't. Sorry.

JOE. You sleep okay?

ELLIE. I slept!

JOE. Good, good.
   I wanted to show you, ah. The pictures, of your great-grandpa, his boat, we talked about the –

ELLIE. Oh – yeah! I wanna see those –

JOE. They're around here somewhere.

(He starts to look.)

ELLIE. Oh – I've got to get going –

(JOE clocks her bag. The sight of it breaks his heart, but he covers.)

JOE. You're leaving? Right now?

ELLIE. Yeah, um.

JOE. Well I can drive you, to the –

ELLIE. It's early, it's okay. I called an Uber.

JOE. A what?

ELLIE. It's a cab but with a regular person driving their regular car.

JOE. *(Suddenly upset.)* You're going to let a stranger drive you to the airport?

ELLIE. I take them all the time. I'm a big girl. Kind of.

JOE. *(Suddenly viscerally upset.)* But I can't have you – I see you for an hour then you're off into the world, God knows where, you're gone.

> (**ELLIE**'s *heart twists and aches.*)

> (**JOE** *takes a breath. Buttons himself back up.*)

ELLIE. Is Roberta –?

JOE. She's still asleep.

> *(Beat.)*

ELLIE. I'm sorry I haven't called more.

JOE. That's alright. I haven't, either.

> *(Beat.)*

ELLIE. Why're we so –

> *(Beat.)*

Why can't we be more –

> *(Beat.)*

JOE. I don't know.

> *(Beat.)*

ELLIE. Do you think she'll be up soon? I don't wanna wake her –

JOE. You'll see her next time.
You want some coffee?

ELLIE. I can grab some there.

> (**ELLIE** *zips her bag shut.*)

JOE. We'll have to come visit you once Roberta's feeling better.

ELLIE. But –

JOE. Once it's warmer.

(Beat.)

ELLIE. Yeah, that'd be great, I'd like that.

*(**ELLIE**'s phone buzzes.)*

My car's here, so.

JOE. Let me help you with your bag –

ELLIE. I'm okay.

(She goes to him. Hugs him.)

*(**JOE** hugs her, restrained.)*

JOE. Okay, bye bye now.

(She starts to go.)

(She stops.)

ELLIE. …See you soon.

*(**ELLIE** grabs her things and goes, leaving **JOE** alone.)*

(He sits on the couch.)

(He looks for his glasses.)

(He tears the place apart.)

JOE. Goddamn glasses –

(He cannot find them. He sits, defeated.)

(The phone rings.)

(He gathers himself, answers.)

Hello.

Yes, this is he.

(Eyes widening, he searches for pen and paper.)

Oh – oh, yes, that'll do – what time is it now?

Yes, we can make it at nine. We will see you there.

*(**ROBERTA** enters, in her pajamas, bathed in peace.)*

Yes. No breakfast.

Alright then. Thank you for – thank you very much.

(*ROBERTA goes to* JOE.)

(*Kisses him.*)

ROBERTA. Good morning, handsome.

(*She eases herself into his arms.*)

Another beautiful day on earth.

JOE. Yes it is!

Have you seen my glasses?

ROBERTA. I haven't.

Did I hear a car?

JOE. Ellie's cab.

ROBERTA. She's gone?

JOE. She didn't want to wake you.

Let's – you need to get dressed.

ROBERTA. Where am I going?

JOE. Dr. Dougherty had a cancellation! They can fit you in at nine.

ROBERTA. Oh –

JOE. You're not supposed to eat before the appointment, but you can have fluids, apple or orange? I'll get your juice while you get dressed. If we leave in ten minutes we'll make it by 9:05. Surely they can wait five minutes. Did you say orange?

ROBERTA. Now just slow down.

We need to talk about what's going to happen.

JOE. Apple?

ROBERTA. I need you to listen to me.

JOE. I'm listening, but sweetheart, we only have a few minutes.

ROBERTA. I don't want to see Dr. Dougherty.

JOE. We said we would get a second opinion.

ROBERTA. *You* / said we would get a second opinion.

JOE. You always get a second opinion.

No one is ever always *right*.

ROBERTA. Is that so?

JOE. Medicine is *inconsistent,* it is sometimes *felt.* Diagnoses are *opinions* that must be weighed against / each other.

ROBERTA. I'm not going to do the treatments.

(Beat.)

JOE. Yes. You are.

ROBERTA. I don't want any of that. I've decided.

I just don't see the point.

JOE. The *point?* The point is to prolong your *life,* the time we have –

ROBERTA. I don't want to spend that time in a microwave! I want to spend it with *you.* The doctor said it might not / even –

JOE. The ONE doctor. Dr. Dougherty has had success with your / type of –

ROBERTA. JOE. LISTEN TO ME.

I don't know how to be here anymore.

It's all too strange. That we eat things. That we digest things. That we shit the things out. That there is mayonnaise, that there are sweet things that there is salt, that we put rings on our fingers and this means that we belong to each other –

JOE. Yes, it's an overwhelming / time, but –

ROBERTA. That you have seen me NAKED, that I write my name on a check and a number and then that I give it to someone and it means anything at all, that there are so many kinds of pens, that I have a middle name, that there is ink, it's all too much.

JOE. Yes and so we must take this one step at a *time.* Apple or orange?

(Beat.)

APPLE. OR. ORANGE.

ROBERTA. Joe I love you – and we still have some time –

JOE. So you are just going to sit back and let it spread, crawl up around your heart, till air can't get through your lungs, until blood can't get to your heart, your brain, until you wither away to bones?! This is your decision?

ROBERTA. Charlie's there.

He's all grown up.

JOE. Oh, come on.

ROBERTA. I knew you would say that.

JOE. What? That you have clearly created a narrative that is comforting to you?

ROBERTA. But so what if I have? What's the harm in believing that I am going somewhere? Who am I hurting?

JOE. ME! It's a goddamn *betrayal!*

ROBERTA. *(Breaking, breathless.)* I am not trying to betray you!

JOE. We agreed! To share a life!

ROBERTA. I know that. But mine is ending.

And I already know where I'm going to go.

JOE. Do I even matter anymore?

ROBERTA. Of course you do. But I'm / going –

JOE. Then please. For the love of the God that you think is there, go get dressed.

We can still make it if we leave now. Get your shoes.

ROBERTA. I'm going to die.

JOE. Fine. I'll get them.

> *(He goes to get her shoes. Brings them to her. Sinks down. Tries to put them on her feet. She resists.)*

ROBERTA. You're gonna die. / I'm gonna die –

JOE. STOP. STOP IT.

ROBERTA. I can't. I am barely here!

JOE. But you ARE!

ROBERTA. You're scared, and that's alright.

JOE. Well of course I am, who isn't?!

ROBERTA. People who know where they're going. Isn't that wonderful?

(**JOE** *dissolves.*)

…I'm going to fix us some French toast. With real butter. Fresh whipped cream.

(*Beat.*)

You want some French toast?

(*Beat.*)

Joe.

(**JOE** *doesn't respond.*)

I know you can hear me.

(*Beat. An old joke:*)

Joe, your hearing aid's off.

(*Beat.*)

"I don't wear a hearing aid."

(*Beat.*)

"I know you don't but sometimes, seems like you do. One that you can turn on and off."

(*Beat.*)

"Yes, well, Bobs, you're blind."

(*Beat.*)

"Blind to what?"

(*Beat.*)

"To all the little ways I see you and I hear you. I see and hear you every day. Every day."

(**JOE** *gets up. He heads toward the front door, not really knowing where he is going.*)

(*And, he leaves.*)

(**ROBERTA,** *alone.*)

News

> (**ELLIE** *returns home with her luggage.*)
>
> (*She pulls off her shoes.*)
>
> (*She lights a cigarette.*)
>
> (*Checks her phone. She checks emails. Texts.*)
>
> (*The news.*)
>
> (*News, news, news.*)
>
> (*Her face grows from boredom to horror to fear to panic.*)
>
> (*She dials. It rings.*)

ELLIE. Hey, it's me. Are you okay? I just saw on the – is that your building?

Will you call me?

Are you okay?

> (*She hangs up. She smokes. She dials again.*)
>
> (*No answer.*)
>
> (*She starts to panic.*)
>
> (*She leaves another message.*)

Could you call me back right now? I'm serious.

Call me back. RIGHT NOW.

> (*She hangs up. Tears start to rise in her throat. She finds her remote, turns on her TV. News of a fire.*)

Fuck.

Fuck.

> (*She pulls on her shoes.*)
>
> (*She heads for the door.*)
>
> (*She opens it to find* **JONAS** *there, waiting, like a ghost, dazed.*)

What –

Are you okay?!

JONAS. I'm okay –

ELLIE. Your building is on FIRE.

JONAS. I *know.*

ELLIE. What happened?!

JONAS. There was a gas leak –

ELLIE. What the FUCK.

JONAS. *I'm* the one who gets to say what the fuck right now!! My *building* is on fire!! What the FUCK!

> (*She throws herself onto his lap, hugging her arms around her neck, tight.*)
>
> (*He moves his arms around her.*)

ELLIE. I thought you were dead –

JONAS. I'm not, I'm not dead.

But I should be, I should be in there right now.

I was supposed to be home.

ELLIE. But you *weren't.* You weren't home.

> (*She kisses his face all over. Burrows into his neck.*)
>
> (*JONAS lets his breath slow, processing everything that just happened.*)
>
> (*As they speak, we see the* **ANGEL** *slowly crossing the apartment.*)
>
> (*There but not. He keeps his eyes forward.*)
>
> (*As he goes, he checks outlets. Blows out candles. Turns off stoves.*)
>
> (*Saves us.*)

JONAS. I was just grabbing a sandwich. I was gonna take it home and eat it. It usually takes like two minutes for them to make it. But there was this new guy working behind the counter and he was intricately slicing everything, layering on the pickles, decorating the bread. And I waited. And then BOOM like the end of the world. We both shook. I went out to look and when I came back – the guy was gone.

> (*This lands on* **ELLIE.**)

(*JONAS* *watches the TV.*)

ELLIE. I can turn this off –

JONAS. No. I wanna see.

(*They watch the news. The fire grows, consuming all that he owns.*)

All my things are in there.

ELLIE. You don't need anything. You can have all of my things.

Everything I have is now yours. Okay?

JONAS. Okay.

(**ELLIE** *takes his hand in hers.*)

(*They watch the news.*)

A Chicken

(JOE *is in an aisle of the grocery store, scanning a shelf intensely.*)

(*He's in his pajama bottoms, tennis shoes, and an overcoat.*)

(*He has a shopping cart containing one sad chicken.*)

(*A* **CHECKOUT BOY** *finds him.*)

CHECKOUT BOY. Can I help you find something, sir?

(JOE *is instantly irked by him.*)

JOE. ...No thank you.

CHECKOUT BOY. Alright, but I happen to know the location of every single item in the store nobigdeal. So.

(*Beat.*)

Nice bird you got there, you could feed a whole family with that.

JOE. Yes, and I intend to.

CHECKOUT BOY. Are you sure I can't help you find anything?

JOE. My wife always gets a particular cornbread mix. It's low sodium. It's in an orange box.

CHECKOUT BOY. I can help you look.

(*The* **CHECKOUT BOY** *stands next to* JOE, *helps him scan.*)

Okay, I see a blue box –

JOE. That's Jiffy, that's not the box. That's not the right kind.

CHECKOUT BOY. Alright, then, is it the Betty Crocker? That's more of a red.

JOE. It's an orange box, I have lived with this woman for TWENTY-NINE YEARS, it's an ORANGE. BOX.

(*Suddenly,* JOE *is in tears.*)

CHECKOUT BOY. Sir – Sir –

JOE. Christ, is this a nightmare?

CHECKOUT BOY. No, sir. It's real.

> *(Beat. JOE wipes his eyes.)*

JOE. What am I going to do –

CHECKOUT BOY. Well you're just gonna follow the directions on the box right here. You're going to add one beaten egg – three teaspoons canola oil –

JOE. No. When she's *gone.*

CHECKOUT BOY. Wait, who're we talking about?

JOE. My wife.

CHECKOUT BOY. Is she going somewhere?

JOE. She's dying.

> *(The words choke him as he says them for the first time.)*

CHECKOUT BOY. Well where is she now?

JOE. She's at home.

> *(Beat.)*

CHECKOUT BOY. Well what're you doing *here*?!

JOE. …What?

CHECKOUT BOY. She's still here! Go hang out with her!

JOE. But I –

CHECKOUT BOY. No! Ever heard of Fresh Direct? It's a website. Get on that. It delivers!

JOE. I just – I needed a minute –

CHECKOUT BOY. Dude.

Go home and be with your wife.

JOE. But she's leaving –

CHECKOUT BOY. But not yet.

> *(JOE processes this.)*
>
> *(He starts to head up the aisle, a lost and broken man.)*

CHECKOUT BOY. Oh – sir?

Are these yours?

> *(He produces* **JOE***'s glasses.)*
>
> *(***JOE*** *nods, dumbfounded.)*
>
> *(The* **CHECKOUT BOY** *places* **JOE***'s glasses into his open hands.)*
>
> *(He puts his glasses back on. He can see.)*

A Reason

> (*Later that night.* **ROBERTA** *is outside where* **ELLIE** *snuck a smoke. She holds an unlit cigarette in her hand. In the other hand, she clutches the landline. Nervously waiting for a call.*)
>
> (*She smokes the unlit cigarette. Remembering.*)
>
> (*Suddenly: the phone rings.*)
>
> (*Her heart leaps.*)

ROBERTA. (*Desperate.*) Joe?

ELLIE. (*Like a child.*) Grandma?
It's Ellie.

> (**ROBERTA** *smiles.*)

ROBERTA. Hi, honey. Sorry. I'm waiting for your grandpa to call.

> (*Beat.*)

ELLIE. I'm sorry I left without saying bye.

ROBERTA. It's okay. I understand. You have your life, you need to live your life.

> (*Beat.*)

ELLIE. Were you sleeping? Did I wake you up?

ROBERTA. No.

ELLIE. Isn't it so weird, that we sleep? That we're alive, but that we need rest to keep living?

ROBERTA. It is, it is.

> (**ELLIE** *reaches for a cigarette, lights it.*)

What is that, are you smoking?

ELLIE. (*Yes.*) No.

> (*Beat.*)

No.

ROBERTA. I know what smoking sounds like, honey, I heard your matchbook. How retro of you. There are lighters, you know.

ELLIE. I like matches. They make me feel like I'm not a computer.

ROBERTA. Are you a computer?

ELLIE. Sometimes.

ROBERTA. Guess what? I'm smoking, too.

ELLIE. You are?

ROBERTA. I didn't light it. I'm mostly just remembering.

ELLIE. Remembering what?

ROBERTA. What it feels like…to think I'm going to live forever.

> *(Beat.)*

ELLIE. I wanted to tell you, um. I believe you, I think. About heaven.

ROBERTA. You do?

ELLIE. I think that there's – and I want there to be – something – more.

> **(ROBERTA** *smiles into the phone.)*

ROBERTA. Me too.

> **(ELLIE** *nods, needing this.)*

Ellie. Put out the cigarette.

> **(ELLIE** *considers.)*

I'll put mine out, too.

> *(They both put their cigarettes out. Together.)*

ELLIE. There. I did.

ROBERTA. Good. Me too.

ELLIE. *(A joke, but not.)* …I think you just saved my life.

> *(A smile grows across **ROBERTA**'s face.)*
>
> *(They sit there together, joined through a suspended line.)*

(Softly, **JOE** *enters, worn out from crying.)*

JOE. What're you doing out here?

*(**ROBERTA** sees him.)*

ROBERTA. *(Into phone.)* Sweetie, could you hold on – don't go anywhere. I'm going to put you on hold.

ELLIE. I don't think that's a thing –

ROBERTA. Hold on.

ELLIE. Oh – okay –

*(**ROBERTA** sets the phone down, and takes him into her arms. They hold each other.)*

JOE. I don't know how to do this.

ROBERTA. No one does.

JOE. I just want to be where you are.

ELLIE. Grandma?

ROBERTA. Oh! Ellie's on the line. I put her on hold.

*(**ROBERTA** goes back to the phone.)*

Ellie, are you still on the line?

ELLIE. Yep, I'm here.

ROBERTA. *(To* **JOE.***)* Say hello to Ellie.

JOE. Alright –

ROBERTA. *(Into phone.)* Ellie, I'm going to give the phone to your granddad, now.

I'll see you soon, alright?

ELLIE. …See you soon.

*(**ROBERTA** holds the phone out to* **JOE,** *and he takes it.)*

JOE. *(Into phone.)* Hello.

*(**ROBERTA** takes his hand.)*

ELLIE. Hi Grandpa!

(He tries.)

JOE. So you made it back alright?

ELLIE. I did.

It wasn't a long flight. I can come back whenever you need.

JOE. Thank you.

(Beat.)

So! You're not a Cubs fan now, are you?

ELLIE. I don't really follow sports.

JOE. Yep, me neither.

ELLIE. I like the snacks though.

JOE. Best part of sports.

ELLIE. I'm pretty into those giant pretzels.

JOE & ELLIE. Except for the mustard.

ELLIE. Exactly!

This guy I'm –

(Beat.)

My boyfriend. He loves mustard. At dinner he *dipped his pizza into it.*

JOE. Your grandma does that!

ELLIE. Lunatics!

(Beat.)

JOE. Ellie. I might, ah. I might need –

ELLIE. I know. I'm here.

(Beat.)

(They smile.)

(Keep talking, connecting.)

*(**ROBERTA** is happy, watching this, and so, eventually, slowly, she slips away.)*

(Leaves couch and husband and granddaughter and floor and chair.)

(Then:)

(She is in heaven. Today, heaven is a clean and glorious diner that smells of pancakes and french fries, with mini jukeboxes at all of the tables that

*gently play the oldies, with the constant whir of
fresh milkshakes being blended.)*

(She sits at a table, perusing a menu.)

(The **ANGEL** *approaches.)*

ANGEL. Welcome back.

> *(***ROBERTA*** looks at him, beaming.)*
>
> *(She holds her arms out to him.)*

ROBERTA. Can I –?

ANGEL. You bet!

> *(He goes to her. And she holds him.)*

ROBERTA. My boy, my boy –

ANGEL. I remember this. This is really nice.

> *(They hold each other, mother and son.)*
>
> *(She holds him at arm's length, looks at him.)*

You hungry?

ROBERTA. Infinitely.

> *(They sit down together, at the booth. They peruse
> menus.)*

What happens now?

ANGEL. This, forever.

ROBERTA. When I learned that in church when I was
young, I couldn't grasp it. The idea of forever. It gave
me a headache. Right here.

> *(She points to her temple.)*

ANGEL. It's confusing, at first. But it settles. You arrive
accustomed to discomfort and time and pain. And
peace itself can be arresting, at first. "What do I look
at?" "Who do I pay?" "Is there a gluten-free option?"
"Where are my pants?" It's hard to be new. But it settles.

> *(***ROBERTA*** nods, trying to let herself settle.)*

ROBERTA. So what's good here?

ANGEL. Uh, everything ever.

(She peruses the menu, which contains everything ever.)

ROBERTA. …How's the waffle ice cream sundae?

ANGEL. There are no words. You have to just try it.

(Waffles appear, drowning in syrup and butter and the purest vanilla ice cream you ever did see.)

*(He feeds **ROBERTA** a bite.)*

(She closes her eyes. Smiles.)

ROBERTA. Tastes like – Vermont.

(Then.)

I remember Vermont.
Half-frozen streams moving past rocks – winding roads
– sharp cheese –
I had a cousin in Vermont.

(She sits, remembering. It doesn't make her sad, she just – remembers.)

I stayed with her when I – when you were –
When I had to go away, after you –

(The thought of it overwhelms her.)

*(The **ANGEL** takes her hand.)*

(Breaking.) I'm so sorry. I was just a person, a young and stupid person. I didn't know grace, or consequence.

ANGEL. But you learned.

ROBERTA. I guess I did.

ANGEL. So it's forgotten.

ROBERTA. But why?

ANGEL. Because you are loved.

ROBERTA. …Joe loved me.

ANGEL. He does. But you are loved beyond his life and yours. You are loved infinitely.

*(**ROBERTA** nods. She settles into this feeling. Lets it be true.)*

ROBERTA. And it just – carries on. Into infinity?

ANGEL. It does.

(She takes his hand, kisses it.)

(She looks out the window.)

ROBERTA. What about the people down there, who –

We want, to –

Who we remember?

ANGEL. …We wait.

ROBERTA. And hope to see them again someday?

ANGEL. Yep. We hope. I did.

ROBERTA. …I can do that.

(Beat.)

Yes, I can do that…

*(**ROBERTA** and the **ANGEL** sit there together, looking out the window.)*

(They share the sundae.)

(They are at peace.)

(They wait.)

End of Play